Salmon and Sockeye
Two Alaska Brown Bear Cubs On a Spring Day Adventure
For Avery ~
Follow
your
dreams
Story and Illustrations by Shawn Rogers
Shawn Rogers
Publication Consultants
Since 1978
PO Box 221974 Anchorage, Alaska 99522-1974

ISBN 978-1-59433-043-8

Library of Congress Catalog Card Number: 2006903544

–First Edition–

MANUFACTURED IN CHINA

For my own sweet cubs—
Fischer, Gunner, and Rivers.

Near the heart of Alaska
In a cave silent and deep
Mama Bear and her cubs
Were cuddled up and asleep.

Protected from snow
Snugly tucked in together
They dreamed of the river
And much warmer weather.

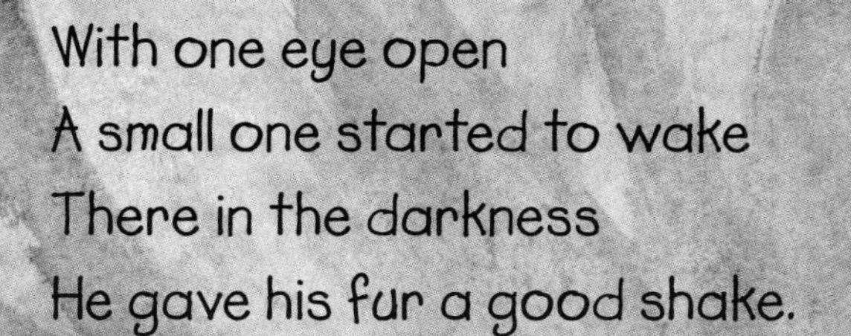

With one eye open
A small one started to wake
There in the darkness
He gave his fur a good shake.

Wiggling and squirming
Big stretch and a yawn
Said the cub to his brother
"Is winter all gone?

"I've slept enough
I'm ready to play
Let's go see if the snow
Has melted away."

"Shhh-I hear you,"
Replied the other,
"But we'll have more fun
If we don't wake Mother."

So quietly the cubs crept
To the door of the den
Outside they saw daisies and
Forget-me-nots again.

With two smiles, a laugh,
And a little bear dance
They ran through the forest
Without a back glance.

Mama Bear kept on sleeping
Oh, how she did snore
Not knowing her babies
Went off to explore.

The two little cubs
Were having such fun
Romping and rolling
In the bright shining sun.

They watched butterflies
Played peek-a-boo in the weeds
They swatted mosquitoes
And discovered new leads.

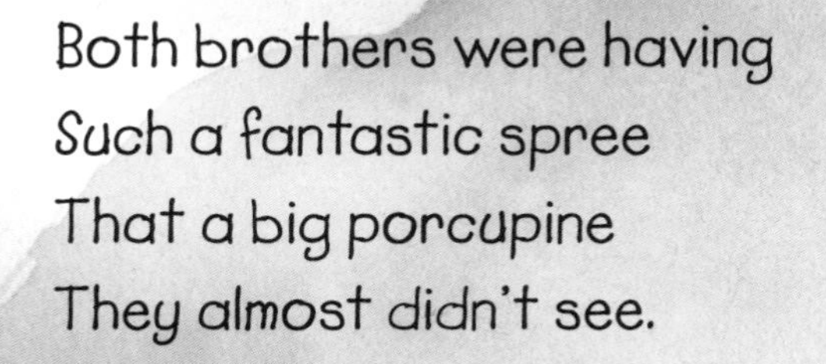

Both brothers were having
Such a fantastic spree
That a big porcupine
They almost didn't see.

Bumping and thumping
They finally stood still
Only inches away
From a very sharp quill.

The porcupine grumbled,
"Whoa, boys—where's the race
Running through the woods
At this crazy pace?

"And why are you guys
Out here all alone?
Does your mother know
You're off on your own?"

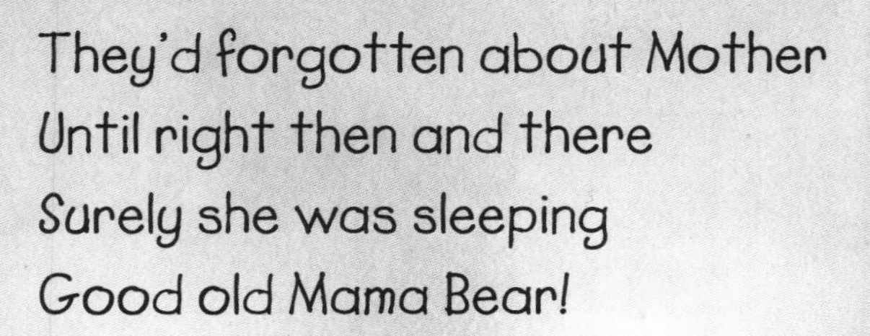

They'd forgotten about Mother
Until right then and there
Surely she was sleeping
Good old Mama Bear!

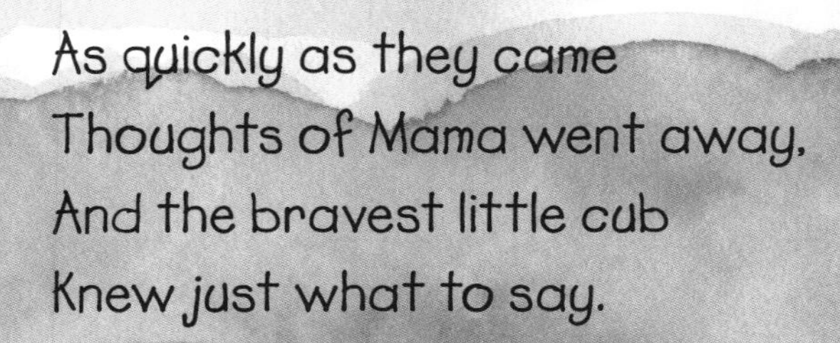

As quickly as they came
Thoughts of Mama went away,
And the bravest little cub
Knew just what to say.

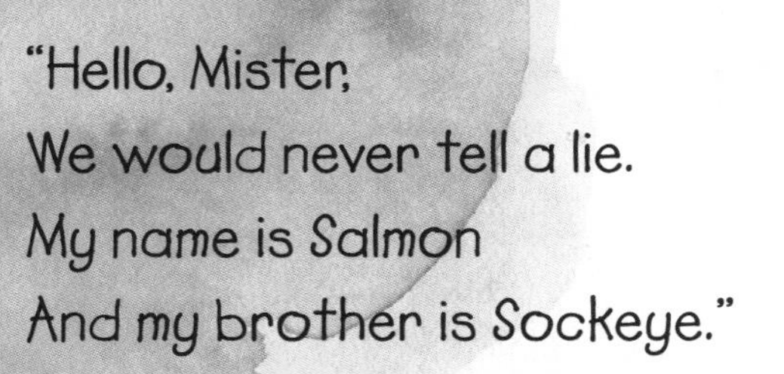

"Hello, Mister,
We would never tell a lie.
My name is Salmon
And my brother is Sockeye."

Confused, the porcupine glared,
"That won't get by me
I don't see fins or scales
And you're not even slimy.

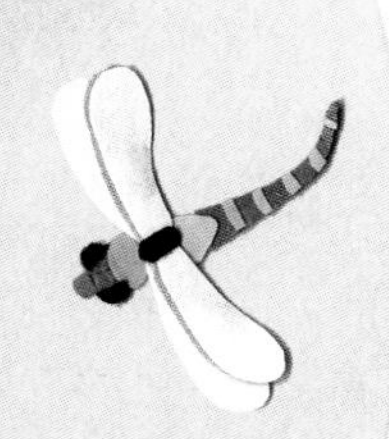

"You think you are fish
Is that what I hear?
No, I'm quite certain
You look like a bear!"

Holding their tummies
The little cubs laughed
Silly old porcupine
He must be daft.

Stopping his giggle
And scratching his brain
Salmon answered,
"Sir, let me explain,

"Yes, of course, we are bears
But we were named after fish
And that is because
It was Mama's wish."

Then Sockeye spoke up
Though usually shy
He looked that prickly fellow
Right in the eye.

"Mama Bear is the best
She's very smart
She's pretty and strong
And has a big heart.

"We love our mommy
And we like our names
I don't mean to be rude
Please excuse me just the same."

Nodding his head
Porcupine chuckled out loud
These were two fine little cubs
To make their mom proud.

"Thanks for clearing that up
You're very polite kids
Now, I must say good-bye"
And with that he did.

As they watched
Their new friend disappear
Sockeye whispered
Into his twin's ear,

"This day has been nice
But will Mama worry?
Let's go back, Salmon
We should hurry."

To this Salmon answered,
"Don't fret,
We can find our way home
No sweat!

"We'll be there before Mom
Even has time to miss us."
And with Salmon so sure
Sockeye felt a little less nervous.

But which way was home
Toward their cave and Mama Bear
Was it this way or that way
Or the worn trail over there?

Using his favorite
Eeny, meeney, miney, moe
Salmon called, "Follow me,
Over here, let's go!"

So with Salmon in command
And leading the search
They looked for their home
Among the spruce and the birch.

For the first time that day
Both cubs were quiet
Listening to the forest
And its animal riot–

A pair of moose calves
Enjoying their first spring
Chatting squirrels, an eagle,
And wolves starting to sing,

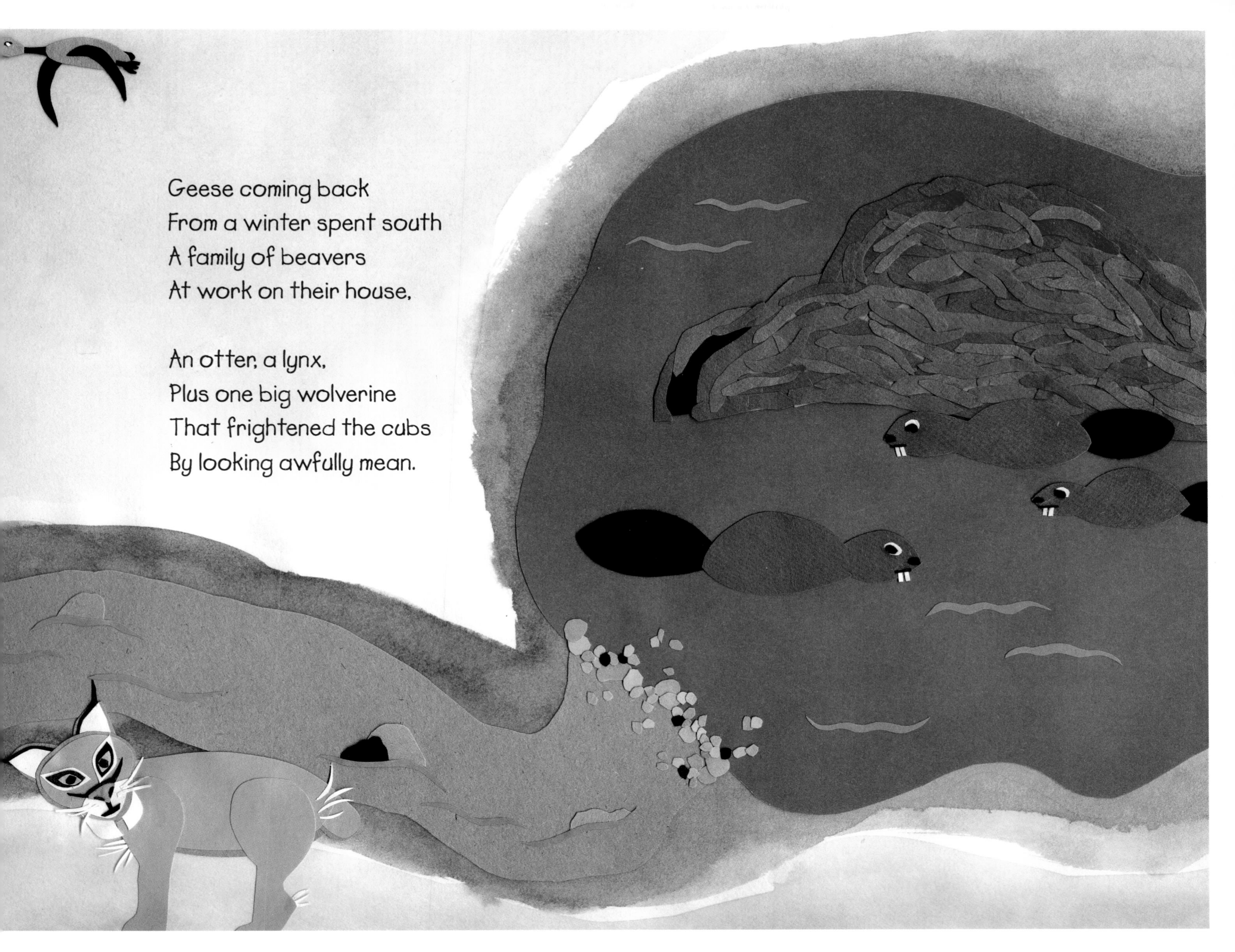

Geese coming back
From a winter spent south
A family of beavers
At work on their house.

An otter, a lynx,
Plus one big wolverine
That frightened the cubs
By looking awfully mean.

The bears had been walking
For nearly an hour
When Sockeye had enough
His mood turning sour.

"I'm scared," he whined,
"I think we're lost.
You don't know where you're going
And I'm sick of being bossed!

"My paws are sore
These shadows are creepy
I want my mom
'Cuz I'm hungry and sleepy!"

That very moment
When Sockeye started to bawl
Mama Bear jerked awake
At her troubled cub's call.

Wasting no time
And quick on her feet
With the speed, skill, and grace
Of an Olympic athlete,

She raced through the woods
Her legs a powerful force
Over rocks and fallen logs
On an obstacle course.

Using her nose
To sniff them out
Mama Bear found the cubs
With her marvelous snout.

They were taken by surprise
When from nowhere she appeared
The sight of their mother
Quickly dried Sockeye's tears.

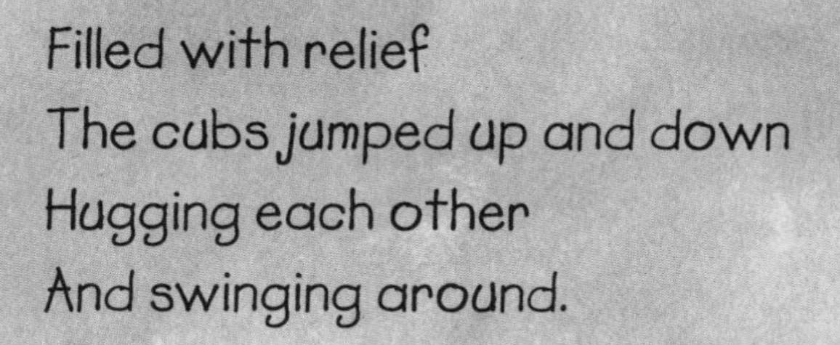

Filled with relief
The cubs jumped up and down
Hugging each other
And swinging around.

Mama Bear was grateful too
For finding her kids in one piece
Giving thanks, she hugged them
Holding tight to their fleece.

When they had all had a good hug
And squeezed another squeeze
Mama Bear spoke softly
Saying, "Boys, listen please...

"I'm very glad
You both are fine,
But, what happened today
Was way out of line.

"You two are young
And didn't intend any harm
Yet there is danger in the woods
That caused me alarm.

"I'm sure it was fun
Playing games along the way
But you shouldn't have left
Without my okay."

Hanging their heads low
The cubs felt bad about their mistake
They understood that running away
Was not a wise choice to make.

"Mom, we're sorry," said Sockeye
And Salmon asked then,
"Can you forgive us
And trust us again?"

Mama Bear nodded
And gave his head a rub
She smiled and said,
"Of course, little cub.

"I want you both to promise
With all the love in your hearts
You'll remember this lesson
As each new day starts:

"Before children run off
There's one important condition
They must ask and receive
Their parents' permission."

"Yes, Ma'am," shouted the cubs,
"You have our guarantee
From now on we'll ask first
You just wait and see."

Mama Bear grinned, "I know you will
Because you're both very clever."
And then she gave them
The best bear hug ever.

Strolling home together
Under the bright northern lights
Mama Bear and her cubs
Happily called it a night.

Facts about Alaska Brown Bears

Alaska is home to 98% of the brown bear population in the United States. There are an estimated 40,000 brown bears in Alaska. The bears are found in almost all areas of the state. Katmai National Park in Southwest Alaska is the largest brown bear preserve in the world. Brown bears, grizzly bears, and Kodiak bears are actually the same species of bears; however, bears along costal areas are often referred to as brown bears, while those in the interior and in northern habitats are called grizzly bears, and bears on Kodiak Island are known as Kodiak bears.

Brown bears hibernate, or sleep through the winter. This usually happens when food becomes hard to find and the weather becomes cold. Bears can spend five to seven months hibernating. Bear-mothers-to-be are the first to enter their winter dens and mothers with new cubs are the last to emerge in the spring. Brown bear cubs are born in the months of January and February. The cubs are born without any hair and weigh less than a pound. A mother brown bear can have anywhere between one and four babies, but twins are the most common.

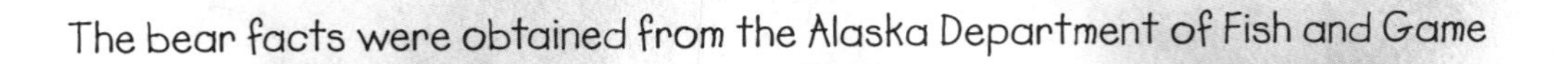
The bear facts were obtained from the Alaska Department of Fish and Game